SECRETS OF THIEF CAVE

CAMP
WANNA BANANA
MYSTERIES

SECRETS OF THIEF CAVE

Becky Freeman

WaterBrook
PRESS

SECRETS OF THIEF CAVE
PUBLISHED BY WATERBROOK PRESS
2375 Telstar Drive, Suite 160
Colorado Springs, Colorado 80920
A division of Random House, Inc.

ISBN 1-57856-350-X

Published in association with the literary agency of Alive Communications, Inc.,
7680 Goddard Street, Suite 200, Colorado Springs, CO 80920.

Printed in the United States of America
2001—First Edition

10 9 8 7 6 5 4 3 2 1

To Trevor St. John Gilbert,
my wonderful nephew and an excellent reader,
who helped me with ideas and encouragement
for this book!

CONTENTS

ACKNOWLEDGMENTS

With gratitude to my agent and friend, Greg Johnson, for recommending me for this project and believing I could write fiction for children. And to Erin Healy, a most delightful and talented editor at WaterBrook who guided, taught, and encouraged me until I finally *became* a children's writer.

To all the children who have brightened my days—my own children (Zach, Zeke, Rachel, and Gabe); my nephews and niece (Tyler, Trevor, and Tori Leigh); my neighborhood bike-riding buddies (Alex, Nicky, and Lindsey); and of course, my first graders (now junior high and high schoolers!) from D. C. Cannon Elementary School.

1

THE JEWEL THIEF

"Jake!" At the sound of his name, Jake Bigsley looked up from the messy maze on the floor of his room and glanced toward the door. His twin sister ran in breathlessly and nearly fell over a stack of cardboard boxes filled with Jake's latest treasures—a grass snake, a toad, and a snapping turtle.

"Hey, be careful there," said Jake, reaching for his pet toad. "You almost smashed Warty."

Joy rolled her eyes and plopped down on the one empty patch of carpet on Jake's bedroom floor.

"What's up?" Jake asked. He kissed Warty's slippery lips and put the little reptile back in its box. He looked at Joy with a smile. She was clutching her throat and making gagging sounds. She always did this when Jake kissed his reptiles and amphibians. Of course, that only made him want to kiss them more, especially when Joy was with her best friend, Maria Garcia. He found something irresistible about making girls gag and squirm. Jake loved to bug his sister —he figured it was a brother's duty.

Joy stopped gagging suddenly as though she remembered why she'd come into Jake's room after all. "Did you go fishing this morning?" she demanded, one eyebrow raised.

"Yes ma'am, I did," Jake answered in his most serious voice. "I confess, I went fishing."

"Ah-HAH!" Joy exclaimed. Her eyes narrowed into suspicious slits, and she pointed at him accusingly. "And what did you use for a fishing lure?"

"I used…I used…, " Jake paused for effect. "I used—a fishing lure!"

"Are you sure?"

"Yep, I'm sure."

"Are you very, very sure?" Joy prodded.

"Okay, Joy," Jake leaned forward with his elbows on his jeans. "What's this all about?"

"I'm missing my antique gold locket—the one Grandma gave me when I was a baby. It's worth a hundred dollars now, but it means way more than that to me. It's an heirloom, you know—a locket of love that's been handed down in the family for generations. Just like Emily's heirloom locket from my *Secret Hope Chest* book. My locket was on my desk last night and now—it's gone!"

Jake thought about asking what an "air-loom" was, but then he decided he really didn't want the long, dramatic explanation that would surely come from his bookworm sister. "And your point is?" Jake countered.

Joy pointed her finger toward Jake's chest. "My point is, I think you used it as a fishing lure!"

"That's *it?* Why would you think I'd go and do a crazy thing like that?" Jake asked as he bent over to pull on his cowboy boots. He did not have time for his sister's imaginative accusations. He reached for his favorite hat—an enormous sombrero—and put it on his head. The Mexican hat had been a gift from his best friend, Marco, who happened to be Maria's twin brother. Jake loved the shade it provided from the hot summer sun, even though it often fell down over his eyes and kept him from seeing where he was going.

Joy took one look at her brother, put one hand on her hip, and said, "Well, hmmm, Jake, I don't know. I mean, how could I possibly think you would do anything crazy? You, the only boy in Tall Pines who wears cowboy boots with shorts. You, the only brother who walks through town—in broad daylight—wearing a yellow Camp Wanna Banana T-shirt down to your knees with a floppy hat as big as a beach umbrella. I just can't imagine how anyone might think you'd do something crazy."

Jake reached up and tipped his sombrero back off his forehead so he could see daylight again. "See what I mean, Joy. You're always jumping to wild conclusions."

Joy drew in her breath slowly as if she were trying to suck a thick milkshake out of a straw. "Of course, dear Jake, there was that time you took my best hair ribbons and safety-pinned raw bacon pieces to them—"

"Hey, they made great little crawdad catchers," Jake replied, brightening at the memory. "Man, me and Marco must have caught us a dozen crawdads in less than fifteen minutes."

Joy pursed her lips and flung both arms toward the ceiling. "And there was also the morning when you took my best satin slip, pinned it around your neck, and tried to jump off the shed like Superman."

"Yeah, but that was when I was a baby."

"Jake, that was last year."

"But I've grown up a lot since then," Jake said, hitching up his shorts as he walked toward the door. "I'm almost a man now. Maybe someday you'll be as mature as—" Sombrero and boxes scattered across the cluttered bedroom as Jake tripped over his Super Squirter water pistol and fell into a pile of slick comic books. He looked up from the floor at Joy sheepishly and decided against finishing his comments.

He had expected Joy to sigh dramatically and roll her eyes. Instead she pointed silently to his hat, which was moving. In fact it was hopping, as if it had suddenly sprung to life. "Warty!" Jake cried as he pounced on the hat to halt his escaped toad. Then Joy *did* sigh. Carefully picking her path through the mess, Joy walked over Jake, the hat, the boxes, and the comic books, flipping her blond ponytail as she left.

"Jake, I want my locket back," Joy announced, "or I'll CLEAN UP YOUR ROOM!"

Jake grimaced at the thought of Joy organizing his beloved treasures, but he wasn't *too* worried. Joy had a tendency to exaggerate everything, turning the smallest problems into movie-sized traumas.

"*Sisters,*" he muttered as he stood up. He didn't have Joy's locket and wasn't going to spend any time trying to figure out why she thought he did. There were more important things to do.

Like find the *real* thief.

Jake picked up Warty and slipped the bumpy-skinned toad into his T-shirt pocket, thinking about the day ahead of him. Nothing spurred Jake to action like the thought of an adventure. Today Joy had given him a mission full of adventure: He and Marco would catch the "air-loom" thief and prove his own innocence!

Grabbing his backpack and sombrero, he walked into the hallway. Jake slung the backpack over his shoulder, careful not to squish Warty. The pack was heavy, loaded with a slingshot, a flashlight, a bottle of water, and a packet of dried peanuts—survival stuff. Jake always thought that true adventurers must be prepared for anything.

"Come on, Warty," Jake said. "We have some detective work to do."

Jake loved Tuesdays. Most summer mornings, Jake and Joy had chores at Camp Wanna Banana, the youth camp where the Bigsley family lived and worked. Jake's job was to fill the bathtub-sized water troughs for the horses and help Señor Garcia, the camp rancher and Marco's dad, clean out the stalls. It was hard work, but Jake loved the horses and knew each one by name. His favorite horse, Brick, was the color of an Arizona sunset. Often he would ride Brick alongside Señor Garcia, helping lead the trail rides.

Joy worked mornings in the camp kitchen. Her job this summer was to pinch off three hundred small pieces from a giant glob of bread dough to make Camp Wanna Banana's famous Monkey Rolls. She'd line the pieces of dough up on steel pans the size of coffee table tops, brush them with butter, cover them with large cloths, and put them on top of the warm oven to rise. Jake's mom would walk over to the camp kitchen at about ten o'clock to start lunch for the campers. By noon, the dining room was filled with the lip-smacking smell of freshly baked bread and the noise of a hundred happy, sweaty, hungry campers. Jake never tired of the smell of hot rolls or the taste of them smothered with butter and Mom's home-made peach jam.

But Tuesdays were free days—no chores! Jake didn't even have to ask Joy were she was going on her day off. He knew she would be heading for her favorite place—the boring, dusty old library. Every Tuesday morning Joy and Maria would walk to Tall Pines Public Library to return their overstuffed bags of books. By that afternoon, the girls would be on the front porch reading through a new stack of books and sipping lemonade like a couple of old ladies.

Let the girls do their sissy stuff, Jake thought as he heard the front door slam behind Joy. *Marco's coming over soon, and we'll have some* real *fun.* At the end of the hall, he peered out a small window that over-looked Lake Willapango to see if he could catch a glimpse of Marco. The Garcias lived just a short canoe ride across the narrow lake. The homes were joined by a longer trail around the shoreline, and the friends sometimes rode bikes to each other's houses. During the summertime, though, they mostly used canoes and paddleboats to ferry themselves back and forth across the lake shortcut. Marco was nowhere to be seen.

Joy's pet spider monkey, Munch-Munch, interrupted Jake's thoughts. Half walking, half hopping down the hall, she spied Jake and hesitated. Jake noticed that Joy had dressed Munch-Munch in a yellow-and-white checked doll dress with—

"Hey! What's that shiny thing in your hairy little hand? Come here, Munchy," Jake said, reaching out his hand. The unusually reluctant monkey jumped toward the stairs with a shriek.

"Hey, Munchy," Jake said again, perplexed by her odd behavior. He grabbed at her tail as she went over the top stair, but she slipped from his hand like a slick banana.

2

SNEAKY CRITTER

"M unch-Munch Bigsley!" Jake hollered as he ran after the speeding monkey. "Stop right now and give me that!"

As Jake jumped the last three stairs, the little creature hopped up onto a high, open windowsill just beyond Jake's reach. She wrapped the edge of the lace curtain around her like an old lady's shawl and blinked her large brown eyes innocently. Jake still couldn't see what Munchy held in her hand, but he could make out that it was small and golden and shimmered in the sunlight. *Very locketlike,* he thought suspiciously.

Then, to Jake's astonishment, Munchy reached out the window and deliberately let the golden object drop into the grass below.

"BAD monkey!" Jake scolded. Munch-Munch hid her face in her hands and tried to hide behind the curtain. Standing on a chair, Jake finally snatched the wriggling pet and marched her back upstairs to the cage in Joy's room. Munchy shook the bars of her cage and began to shriek.

"I know you want to come out and play," Jake said sternly and loudly over the noise of the screaming monkey. "But you have to learn to obey—and not take things that don't belong to you. You'll have to stay in your cage today."

At this Munch-Munch stopped her screeching and lay down on her back with her feet up in the air. She curled her small toes around the slim metal bars of the cage, then grabbed her "blankie" and pulled it over her face. She looked so quiet and sad and funny with her feet sticking up and her face under the doll-sized blanket that Jake almost walked over to rescue her from her punishment. The whole family loved this little spider monkey; in fact, Camp Wanna Banana had been named in her honor. But Jake knew she'd never learn to obey if he gave in simply because she looked so cute.

Now to find the locket and get Joy off my back, Jake thought. He ran down the stairs once more and then toward the back door, pausing only to wave at his mother and gulp down a quick glass of milk as he passed by the kitchen counter.

"Where are you off to in such a hurry?" Mom asked as she stirred a thick spoonful of fresh cream into her morning cup of coffee. "Goin' to hang out with the Twiblings?" Jake's mom had begun calling the two sets of twins—Marco and Maria, and Jake and Joy—"the Twiblings," a combination of the word "twins" and "siblings." Jake thought it sounded silly at first, but he was used to his mother making up crazy words, and now he kind of liked being a Twibling.

"Not right now," Jake said after his last swallow of milk. "I'm going to prove that Joy's locket was stolen by a hairy, twelve-inch-tall jewel thief!"

3

DETECTIVES ON DUTY

"Eh, *chico.* What's so funny?" The question came from a boy about the same age as Jake. Other than the fact that Marco Garcia had brown skin and dark eyes, while Jake was blond and fair, the boys could have been brothers. Both were skinny and had hair that stood up like wild, uncut grass. And both wore clothes that always seemed too big. Their large T-shirts and baggy shorts hung like heavy drapes on their small, thin bodies.

Jake turned toward his friend, still laughing softly.

He stood in the grass below the window where Munch-Munch had thrown away the locket. Only it hadn't been a locket after all.

"What are you holding there?" Marco asked as he walked toward his best friend.

"A bunch of Golden Nugget candy-bar wrappers, wadded up in a foil ball," Jake answered. "I found it behind this rock on the grass."

"Well, where's the candy?" Marco asked, his eyes lighting up at the thought of sweets.

"The chocolate bars are in the tummy of a bad little monkey. And from the size of this golden ball of wrappers, I'm guessing she's a monkey with a pretty big stomachache. No wonder she was acting so miserable."

"Munchy?"

"Yep. At first I thought Munch-Munch had taken Joy's missing gold locket. But she must have taken a fistful of candy bars from the Camp Wanna Banana snack bar while we weren't looking. She threw the wadded-up wrappers out here when I found out her secret." Jake carelessly dropped the ball of wrappers back to the ground, and it rolled to a stop behind the rock where he'd found it.

Jake's mom stuck her head out the screen door. "Jake!" she called. "Have you seen my wedding ring? I put it on the windowsill while I was washing dishes last night—and now it's gone!"

"No, Mom!" Jake yelled back. "But we'll help you look for it, okay?"

"Thanks, hon," she said, disappearing back into the house. Her voice floated out through the kitchen window. "I'll let you know if I find it first."

"That's the second piece of jewelry missing today," Jake said to Marco in a low voice. "We've got our work cut out for us. It appears there's a jewel thief on the loose."

Marco nodded seriously. Then, putting his arm around Jake's skinny shoulders, he said, "This is a job for…"

"Dos Amigos!" the boys finished in unison. The cry startled Warty, who nearly jumped out of Jake's pocket.

Both boys dug around in the pockets of their shorts, and each produced a long green sash. As Jake returned Warty to his shirt pocket, he noticed that Warty and the sash were nearly the same color. Marco and he had found the sashes, covered in Girl Scout badges, at the Tall Pines Goodwill two weeks ago. After removing the badges, they had written "Dos Amigos Detective Agency" across the strips of green fabric with a bright yellow paint pen.

Jake and Marco had worn their matching detective sashes, slung sideways across one shoulder, when they walked together into the public library last Tuesday to surprise their sisters. But Joy and Maria hid in the stacks, pretending they didn't know their own brothers.

"What's the matter with you?" Jake had whispered to Joy when he finally found his sister crouched behind a giant teddy bear in the children's reading nook. "Don't you want to be part of our detective agency? Don't you want to figure out unsolved mysteries?"

Joy had rolled her eyes before answering, "Jake, you *are* an unsolved mystery. Hey, I have a great idea—why don't you two go undercover for a while?"

"Yes," said Maria, who was squatting behind a small wooden table. "Why don't you take off your sashes so the enemy won't suspect who you are!"

Marco and Jake had agreed that the girls had a point, so they stuffed the sashes into their pockets. But sometimes, when they were pretty confident no criminals were around, Jake and Marco would bring out the sashes and put them on.

This was one of those times. After draping their detective sashes across their chests, the two boys marched down the Willapango Trail that led from the Bigsleys' home into the woods near Camp Wanna Banana. With their shoulders back and their heads held high, Jake found himself thinking how brave and brilliant he and Marco must look.

But try as he might to keep a serious, soldierlike expression as he marched, Jake's face had a hard time hiding the excitement bubbling up in his heart. He had a *real* mystery to solve and, well, this was just the sort of adventure Jake lived for.

Marco paused near a pine tree, stood at attention, and asked, "Where to now, Detective Jake?"

Jake pivoted around, clicking the heels of his cowboy boots together. "First, we check out the Camp Wanna Banana perimeter to see if anyone looks suspicious. Then let's head over to the Treetop Meeting House to get a good look around from up high. Hey, I wonder if we can borrow some binoculars from Mr. Fields over at the nature center?"

Mr. Fields was the science teacher at Tall Pines

Junior High School during the school year, but this summer he had opened a small nature center for Camp Wanna Banana campers. Mr. Fields loved kids, and he loved God's creation as well. Some wealthy scientists from Arizona who also loved kids and God's creation had started a ministry called God's Natural Treasures. One of the many good things God's Natural Treasures did with their money was to pay Mr. Fields's summer salary at Camp Wanna Banana. So Mr. Fields was sort of a summer scientist-missionary to kids. Jake liked how the teacher was always looking out for God's miracles, or "GMs," as he called them. Anything from a rainbow to a roach might be a GM to Mr. Fields. He always kept neat science stuff around, things boys like Jake loved: bugs in jars, pond scum on microscope slides, bird-watching binoculars, and so forth.

Mr. Fields's camp office was really an old abandoned cabin—the one that the Twiblings had discovered in the late spring—on the other side of Lake Willapango, not far from the Garcias' house. The friends had wanted to keep it for a clubhouse, but they'd been content with a compromise: Mr. Fields could use it during summer camp sessions, and the

Twiblings could have it as a clubhouse during the school year.

"Let's stop by after we check out the camp," Marco said. "Then we can take the binoculars up to the tree house and have a good look around."

The boys had reached a high spot in the trail. Camp Wanna Banana lay beneath them, and the woods climbed the hill behind them. *The trees will provide good cover,* Jake thought. He pulled out his water bottle to take a swig and survey the scene.

Marco drank too and then paused, bottle in hand, with a sudden thought. "Jake," he wondered aloud, "what will we do with the thief if we *do* catch him?"

Jake took the bottle back and tucked it away securely in his backpack before stepping off the path. "Just follow, watch, and learn, Marco," said Jake as he marched on through the thick leaves into a dirt clearing. "Follow, watch, and lear—"

But Jake could not finish his sentence because he was too busy falling, headfirst, into darkness.

4

VOICES

M arco!" Jake called from the bottom of the shallow, dark pit. "Help! Everything is upside down!"

"Well," observed Marco as he peered down at his friend, "that's not exactly true. Not everything is upside down. *You* are actually the only thing that is upside down. All I can see is the bottoms of your cowboy boots."

"Pull me outta here!" Jake hollered, though his voice sounded distant and muffled even to himself.

Jake felt around the dirt surrounding him. The hole appeared to be about as wide as his bunk-bed mattress and much deeper. Marco stood up and leaned over the hole, trying to grab at Jake's flailing boots, but then Marco lost his balance and fell into the hole as well. Soon they were both jumbled up together like two wriggling puppies.

"Some detective you are!" said Jake in disgust.

"Hey, you fell in first," Marco answered in frustration as he and Jake got themselves right side up again. They were covered with loose soil. As they stood upright, they could see that the top of the hole was about a foot higher than their heads. Jake started to give Marco a boost when he heard the voices of men talking nearby.

"Shhh," whispered Jake. "Maybe it's the jewel thief!"

"Sounds more like jewel *thieves*," Marco whispered back. "I think there's two of them."

"*Shhh!*" Jake repeated. "Put your head down and listen."

The boys both went silent.

"Hey, Ricky," the gruff voice of an older man said, "did you get that hole dug for the soil test?"

"Yes sir," a younger voice answered in reply. "Soil looks good and firm. Perfect foundation for your logging warehouse and sawmill. And the lake will come in handy for floating the cut trees. If you can get Bigsley to sell that kids' camp, that is. He's pretty partial to it, I hear."

The older man snickered. "Oh, I'll get him to sell it all right, Ricky. Money speaks louder than monkey business, and besides, taxes have him in a real bind. They doubled this year, and there's no way I can see that he'll get the money before the bank takes over. Within a year, this little wilderness camp for rug rats is going to be Tall Pines Lumber Yard, and we'll make some real use of these trees."

Jake could feel the heat of anger rising in his face, but he somehow managed not to shout, "My dad will *never* let you cut down these beautiful trees!" He realized too late, however, that he'd forgotten to stifle something else.

"Riiiibit."

"Pardon me?" the voice of the older man said.

"I didn't say anything, sir," answered Ricky.

"Riiibbbbbbbiiiiit."

Jake desperately tried to cover Warty's throaty

noises by holding his hand over his shirt pocket. But Warty was ready to sing, and there was nothing Jake could do but hold his breath and pray.

"There's some sort of noise coming from that hole you dug," the gruff voice said. "Take a look in there, Ricky."

Jake could feel his heart pounding in his chest—but whether it was from anger or fear or both, he didn't know. He could feel Marco shaking next to him as the heavy steps got closer. Jake tried his best to look invisible.

5

JAKE ATTACK

Well, well," said the voice that belonged to the man named Ricky. "I see three pairs of eyeballs lookin' at me."

"What's that you say?" asked the other man.

"Yep, two sets of eyes belong to boys, and one set belongs to a startled toad. Hey, what are you kids doing in there?"

"We were…uh…we were…uh…," Marco's voice was coming in starts and sputters like the cold engine of the old camp truck.

Jake took over, finally clearing his own throat of the fear stuck in it. It was awkward for Jake to crane his neck to meet the eye of the six-foot-tall Ricky—especially from his position below ground level. Nevertheless, Jake gave it his best shot. "We were just walking in the woods, and we fell in this hole," Jake said. Then with an edge of accusation he added, "A hole that *happens* to be on *my dad's* property."

"Oh, yeah? And who is your dad?" Ricky asked.

"Kevin Bigsley, and he's bigger than a pine tree and stronger than a backhoe, and he'll never sell Camp Wanna Banana in a million years."

Ricky chuckled, then reached down to pull each boy out of the pit with one heave of his muscled arms. "Boys, I'm Rick Zane, a geologist. I'm out here with Mr. Bob Grant." Rick gestured toward the man with him. "He's the president of Woodland State Bank."

Though Rick was strong and rough, Jake noticed a certain kindness in his eyes that calmed Jake's anger just a little bit. But Jake disliked Mr. Grant at first sight. Jake took a long, disapproving look in the banker's direction. He thought the man looked like a well-dressed tadpole out of a pond, flopping around the woods in his fancy suit and silk tie. The banker's face was tight, his lips drawn, like he'd just taken a bite of a lemon. Jake wondered if grownups like Mr. Grant could ever have been kids. *Real* kids, that is, who like dirt and adventure more than wearing ties and acting important.

"Mr. Grant," Jake started slowly. But then something clicked in his head, something that felt like white-hot anger, and he began to pour out all his thoughts without pausing to think first. "Mr. Grant, I heard what you said about trying to make my dad sell the camp so you can put a bunch of ugly old buildings on our land. Have you ever met my dad? Because if you ever met my dad, you'd know that he'd rather be a plump turkey on Thanksgiving Day than give up this beautiful land and this camp for kids to a sour-faced old banker like *you*." Jake had to take a deep breath after spitting out such a long sentence.

Mr. Grant laughed. "Your father," he said in a voice as cold as crushed ice, "has very little choice in the matter. And you, young man, are decidedly rude." The banker turned his back on the boys and spoke to Rick. "Let's go."

"Okay, sir. I've finished my job here. Don't forget

to pick up your watch," Rick said as he gathered up a roll of important-looking papers. Rick turned toward Jake and apparently noticed the question on the boy's face. "He took the watch off earlier to avoid getting dirt in it," Rick said by way of explanation.

Mr. Clean and Mean, Jake thought. And then again something inside him burst like a balloon too full of air.

With the boldness of a crazed gorilla, Jake stuck out his chest and shouted in Mr. Grant's direction, "We are the Dos Amigos! And we'll fight you to the death for our land!"

Marco looked over at Jake, and his eyes grew as wide as two raccoon rings. "Jake—are you *loco?*"

But Jake was far too upset to pay attention to Marco's protests.

Without hesitation, Jake marched over to Mr. Grant and gave him a quick, swift kick in the shins with the point of his cowboy boot. Then, flailing wildly, he tried to karate chop Mr. Grant's outstretched arms. Rick and Marco had to pull the furious Jake off the bewildered banker.

Once Mr. Grant was free of the kicking, chopping, shouting Jake, the banker stood back, brushed the dirt off his suit, scowled at Jake, and said, "Tell your father I'll call him tonight about your little temper tantrum. And I'll be seeing him in town soon. We have business to discuss."

Marco tugged at Jake's arm and said, "Calm down, Jake. Come on, let's get out of here."

Jake turned to walk out of the woods with Marco. His green Dos Amigos sash had become dirty and torn in the scuffle and looked the way Jake's insides felt—ripped apart and sickly green.

Jake looked back once more at the banker, the man who wanted to take away Jake's family home and Camp Wanna Banana and his forest full of adventure. Then with all the feeling he could muster, he left the scene with the meanest words he could think of. "Mr. Grant, sir. I don't like you, and I don't like your shirt."

6

STARLIGHT CHAT

J akc explained what happened as best as he could as
soon as his dad came home from working at Camp
Wanna Banana. He was grateful that his father didn't
yell at him for trying to karate chop Mr. Grant,
although he did make Jake promise to go with him to
the bank to apologize. "Son," his father had said, "if
you don't learn self-control, you won't become the
strong, brave young man you really want to be."

When Jake asked what self-control had to do with
being strong and brave, his father simply replied,

"Sometimes the most courageous thing a man can do is to say nothing and walk quietly away." Jake had never really thought about that. In most of the action movies he loved, the heroes just kicked and punched the bad guys into giving up.

Supper was especially quiet that night. Few words were spoken over the simple bowls of steaming stew and squares of cornbread. Jake figured Dad was worried about taxes, Mom was sad about her missing wedding ring, and Joy was sighing dramatically over the loss of her "air-loom" locket. As for himself, Jake was confused about the events of the day and Mr. Grant's plans to take over the camp.

After dinner Jake finally felt like talking with his father. While Joy and Mom and Munchy chatted and washed the dishes, Jake found his dad sitting on the front porch fiddling with the fishing line on his favorite reel and occasionally looking at the stars. They looked like tiny fireflies, hundreds and thousands of them scattered across a black velvet sky.

"Dad, you aren't ever going to sell our house and Camp Wanna Banana, are you?"

Jake's dad set down the reel and picked up a rod. "I don't want to, no. I never want to sell this property. It seemed, a few years ago, that this land was like a gift from God to be used to tell other kids about His love, to let them see how beautiful His world is out here in nature…"

"And to have lots of fun," Jake added solemnly.

Dad smiled, thinking of all the kids he'd watched that day at Camp Wanna Banana—sliding down the banana slide, jumping in the Monkey Jumping Hut at Banana Bash Zone, and singing praises to God from the Treetop Meeting House. "Yes, Son, and to have lots of fun."

"Then why did Mr. Grant say you have no choice?"

"Jake, we have a big tax payment due on our property. Right now I do not know how we can possibly pay it."

"I'll earn the money by mowing lawns!" Jake eagerly offered.

"I'm afraid it's more money than you or I can come up with even in a whole year of mowing lawns."

"I can do it; I know I can!"

"Jake," Mr. Bigsley said, "listen to me. Look up at the sky. See how high it is? No matter how tall you are, or how tall I am, neither of us can touch the stars.

Some problems are like that, Son. They are bigger than anything you or I can solve."

"But God can solve them."

"You know, Jake, He sure can. But you have got to realize that you can't fix everything, can't solve everything. You and I both, we men, have to learn to give our problems to God in prayer."

"If we pray, will God give us the money to save Camp Wanna Banana?"

"I don't know that for sure, Son. He might just do that. But He may have other plans for our family, and that's okay too. Because we will only be happy if we are following God's directions."

"Can I pray?" Jake asked.

"Sure," Dad answered as he slipped his arm around his son's narrow shoulders and bowed his head.

"Dear God," Jake began. "Dad and me, well, we've got a problem that is way too big for us. We've tried, but we can't figure out what to do. I guess that kicking mean ol' Mr. Grant in the shins isn't helping much either. Tomorrow I hope I feel sorrier for that than I do tonight. Help me to trust You to work everything out, no matter what happens. In Jesus' name, amen."

Right after Jake's "amen" the phone rang. True to his word, it was Mr. Grant, calling to talk about that afternoon's incident. Jake's mom brought the cordless phone out on the porch so her husband could take the call without coming inside. "Yes, Mr. Grant," Jake overheard his dad say. For a while his father just listened quietly. Then Jake saw his father's right eye twitch. Dad's right eye only twitched when he got really mad.

"Look, Mr. Grant," he said at last. "Jake lost his temper with you today, and for that he is sorry and will apologize. He was scared and hurt, and I hope you can understand how a boy afraid of losing his home and the land he loves might strike out. But Jake would never, never steal anything. That's the end of our conversation tonight. I'll see you day after tomorrow for our appointment."

Jake sat up, his eyes wide. "What did Mr. Grant say I took?" Jake asked.

"His gold watch. He took it off and put it on a log in the woods where you were today. He's convinced you stole it."

"Dad, I didn't—"

"I know, Son."

Jake was silent for a moment before speaking again. "But I think I might know who did."

"Who?"

"The same jewel thief that stole Mom's ring and took Joy's locket, that's who. And me and Marco are going to catch him!"

"Going to do it all alone are you, just the two of you?"

Jake smiled softly and lowered his voice. "I mean, with God's help, we'll catch the thief—if it's what He wants us to do."

7

THE TRADE

ake," Joy called to her brother from the porch swing at the side of the house, one of her favorite reading spots. "Do you think God's going to help Dad get the money to save Camp Wanna Banana?"

"I don't know, Joy," Jake said. He was sitting on a nearby rock whittling an old stick. Recent events had made him less interested in adventure than usual. "But I'm sure praying hard. Maybe He'll rain down pennies from heaven!"

Joy laughed. "It would take a one-foot pile of pennies, filling the whole camp, to pay off the taxes we owe." Her face turned suddenly sad and serious. "Jake, I don't want to leave this place. I love it here! And I finally have a real friend in Maria. I don't think I could stand it if we have to leave."

Jake stopped whittling and looked up at his sister. "I know, Joy. I know. " He glanced down at the grass nearby, looked up thoughtfully and said, "Hmmm… that's interesting."

"What's interesting?" Joy asked.

"I dropped that ball of gold foil candy wrappers behind a rock over here yesterday, and now it's gone," Jake said. He stood up to give the area a closer inspection.

Joy put her book down on the swing and walked over to where Jake was searching. She bent over to pick up something, and Jake saw it flash in the sunlight.

"Looks like your jewel thief made a trade," she said. "He left a gold watch in its place."

"Oh NO!" Jake shouted, taking the watch from Joy. "This must be Mr. Grant's watch! How in the world did it get here? *Great.* Joy, what am I gonna do? If I give it back, he'll think I really *did* take it."

Joy shook her head thoughtfully. "Jake, this is so weird. Why would a thief leave the watch and take the candy wrappers instead?"

"I only wish I knew," he said, scratching his head until a little tuft of yellow hair stood up on end. "What am I gonna do? I'm not sure even Dad would believe it was a coincidence."

Jake started pacing. "Maybe somebody wanted to make me look guilty, wanted to make it look like I stole the watch. But who? And why?"

Joy walked over to the porch swing and sat in silence for a minute. Jake kept pacing and scratching, trying to sort out the puzzle in his head.

"Did anyone else know about where you dropped the ball of foil?" Joy finally asked. "And who was with you during that run-in with Mr. Grant? Could anyone you know have taken the watch?"

Suddenly Jake's face turned from confusion to sadness to disbelief. There was only one person who fit Joy's description. "Joy," Jake finally answered. "Marco Garcia has to be the jewel thief."

Joy blinked in surprise. "Oh no, Jake, why would he do such a thing?"

"I don't know," said Jake. He placed the gold watch in his backpack and reached to grab his trusty sombrero from a peg on a nearby tree. "But come on. You and I are going to find out!"

8

TWIBLING TROUBLE

Within fifteen minutes, Jake and Joy had run down to the water's edge and paddled their canoe across the lake to where Marco and Maria Garcia lived. Señora Garcia opened the cheery red door of the family's two-story white brick home. Her dark hair was piled up in a bun of licorice-colored braids, and her black lashes had a light dusting of corn flour on them.

"Come in, Twiblitos," she said with a smile, speaking her own Spanish version of the twins' nickname. She pointed toward the kitchen, where the air was rich with the smell of fresh tortillas. Jake took off his sombrero and set the backpack down by the door. Señora Garcia offered Jake and Joy warm tortillas slathered in fresh, creamy butter before calling upstairs for Marco and Maria to come down.

The Garcia twins appeared at the same time, and soon the four friends were eating tortillas and drinking tall glasses of cold milk—or *leche frio,* as the Garcias called it—around the bright red-and-yellow tiled kitchen table. Normally Jake couldn't resist Señora Garcia's homemade wonders, but today he found himself distracted. The bites of tortilla balled in his throat as he tried to think of a way to confront his best friend, and swallowing was difficult. He didn't say much.

When Señora Garcia finally left the kitchen to check on her marigold garden, Jake put down the butter knife, looked at Marco and asked bluntly, "So why'd you do it?"

Marco looked as though he'd swallowed a fly.

"Why'd I do *what?*" he asked.

"Don't pretend to be so innocent," Jake said, going quickly from sad to angry. "I know that you took Mr. Grant's watch. What I don't know is why—

and why you took the gold wad of candy wrappers as well. They aren't worth anything."

Maria looked shocked. Marco looked as if he'd been kicked in the stomach. "Jake Bigsley!" he shouted. "I am your best friend. You know me as well as anyone. How could you even think I'd steal something—much less blame it on you?"

Immediately Jake looked at Joy and then looked down. Finally Jake spoke up and explained why they suspected Marco.

Marco listened quietly until tears of hurt and anger pooled in his eyes. "Jake, I didn't do it."

And Jake could tell, from this look of sadness and betrayal on his friend's face, that Marco was telling the truth. Jake had made a terrible mistake.

"Marco," Jake said, reaching for his friend's arm. "Please forgive me. It's just that so much has happened in the past two days. Dad tells me I need to learn to slow down and pray before I talk. And before I kick and karate chop. I wonder sometimes if I'll ever learn."

Marco nodded and gripped Jake's hand the way football players do when they come off the field after a good play—or a bad one. It was a cross between an arm-wrestling hold and a handshake.

"It's okay, chico. I forgive you."

"Amigos?" Jake asked.

"Amigos," Marco replied with a smile.

The phone rang, startling the Twiblings out of their private moment. Maria got up to answer it. Her eyes grew wide.

"What's the matter?" Joy asked in a whisper.

Maria handed the phone to Jake. "It's your dad," she told him.

Jake took the phone from Maria. "Hello?" Jake asked. His voice quivered on the "lo" part of his greeting.

"Jake," Dad said, his voice a mixture of anger and worry. "Mr. Grant just called me. He said one of his men from the bank was walking up to our house about an hour ago, on his way to deliver some papers to me, when he saw you holding Mr. Grant's gold watch. Instead of coming to our door, he turned around, drove back to the bank, and reported what he saw to Mr. Grant. What's going on, Son?"

Jake could think of nothing to say for a long time. Finally he said, "Dad, I'm innocent, but I don't know how to prove it to you yet. Give me some time, and I'll explain it all."

"Jake, you have until the end of the day." After a brief, confused exchange of good-byes, Dad hung up on the other end.

Jake gulped. "I'm toast," he croaked.

"What?" the three friends asked all at once.

"One of Mr. Grant's workers saw me with the watch and called Dad," Jake said flatly. He told them what his dad had said.

Maria downed the last bit of her milk and set her glass on the table with conviction. "Then, come on, amigos. We have six hours of daylight to catch the real thief."

"Just one minute," said Joy as she turned toward Jake. "I really want to help solve this mystery and get you off the hook. But I want to make one thing perfectly clear: Maria and I are *not* going to wear any detective sashes—ever. Okay? And we don't want to be seen in public with you guys wearing them either."

"Fine with me," Jake answered. "No sashes." He wasn't in the mood to wear his own sash anyway. He solemnly picked up his backpack and placed the sombrero firmly on his head before leading the group out the front door toward Camp Wanna Banana.

9

ENCHANTED FOREST AND CANDY-WRAPPER CLUES

W"here are we going?" asked Maria as she ran to catch up with the other three friends.

"We're returning to the scene of the crime," Jake said as he motioned toward the waiting canoe. "Jump in."

When the four amigos landed on the other side of the lake, they climbed out and looked to Jake, their fearless leader in a giant sombrero, for direction.

He stood up tall and walked over to a tree, almost hitting his head on a low branch. "We're going back to the spot where Marco and I saw Mr. Grant, but I want to take another path through the woods," he said, pointing into the thick growth beyond the tree. "We'll be making our own trail. I don't want to run into Dad or any campers or any of Mr. Grant's workers until we figure out who's stealing all the gold jewelry."

"And candy wrappers," added Marco.

"Yes," said Jake. "And candy wrappers."

"This is one weird thief," Maria added.

As they walked, Jake started pulling leaves and colorful berries off of nearby bushes and tucking them into the band of his sombrero. "Good thing we're weird detectives," Joy said, waving her hand in Jake's direction. "Or at least one of us is, for sure."

Jake ignored his sister's comment and pressed ahead, pushing tree branches out of his way as he went. He figured she was just jealous of his unique style. But Jake's thoughts were distracted by something he spied out of the corner of his eye. It was a clearing heavily layered with dried leaves and grass and moss.

"Hey," Jake said. "Come over this way. I've never seen this part of the forest before."

He stepped into the clearing and felt the ground

give way under his boots. Not all the way, however. It wasn't like stepping into a covered hole or even into a pile of leaves. It was more like the strangest feeling of walking on a dirt-covered trampoline.

"Whoooaa!" Jake yelled as he bounce-walked his way to the center of the clearing. "Cool!"

"Jake!" Joy yelled. "Be careful—what if you're walking into quicksand!"

"No," said Jake, "it's not quicksand. It's not like anything I've ever walked on before in my life. Come try this!"

Within minutes the four friends were walking around on the spongy ground, their eyes wide in amazement. The leaves filtered the sunlight, which danced on their heads and gave the whole scene an almost magical sparkle. "Oh, wow! Look at that patch of brightly colored flowers! It's like finding an enchanted spot in the forest!" Joy called to Maria.

"Like Camelot!" answered Maria as she walked on the bouncing ground in the glow of midafternoon. Jake knew that his sister was daydreaming of knights and castles and princesses from her favorite stories.

"What's that?" asked Marco, pointing to a path ahead of them.

Jake stopped bouncing and went to take a closer look. He stared in wonder.

"It's pennies," he said in a near whisper.

Joy caught up to her brother and stopped. Jake could not believe his eyes. Pennies, dozens of pennies, were strewn along the dusty dirt path leading out of the clearing.

"Are you thinking what I'm thinking?" Joy asked Jake.

Jake nodded slowly and looked toward the sky, as he said, "Pennies from heaven." He felt the rush of adventure take hold of his pounding heart. "Let's follow the penny trail," he said, plunging ahead.

Joy, Marco, and Maria followed behind Jake in hushed silence as he led them along the forest floor littered with copper pennies.

"Oh my goodness," Jake said, reaching for something on the ground. "Look at this." He held a piece of golden foil up to the light.

"Is it a Golden Nugget candy-bar wrapper?" Marco asked.

Jake nodded.

"Is there any chocolate left in it?" Marco asked hopefully.

Jake shook his head. The Twiblings kept walking. Along the way they discovered more golden wrappers, a few nickels, some silver nails and bolts, and brightly colored pieces of glass.

"This is spooky," said Joy after they'd walked for a while. The afternoon light grew dim as the trees overhead grew thicker with leaves and heavy branches. "I think we ought to go home now."

"Are you crazy?" asked Jake. "This is amazing! We should be closing in on the thief anytime now."

"Exactly why I want to go home," said Joy. "He could be dangerous. I'm not having fun anymore. I think I'm about to have a panic attack instead."

"Don't be so dramatic," Jake said. "You've been reading too many books." Suddenly Jake stopped and stared. The sight before him was an adventurer's dream come true.

"What is it?" Marco asked.

"A cave!" Jake shouted back. "We have a real cave on our land! Let's go in!"

"No, Jake, don't!" Joy yelled.

But Jake wasn't about to be stopped by his dramatic sister. He ducked out of the sunlight into the dark, yawning mouth of the cave.

10

DARK SHADOWS

As Jake walked into the cave and around a small bend he was surprised by the sudden and complete absence of light. He could not see his own hand in front his face—and this time, it wasn't just because his sombrero had fallen down on his head. He was glad he'd remembered to bring his detective backpack along. He took it off, managed to unzip it, and groped around inside for his emergency flashlight. A sudden scuffle and scratching and scurrying sound drew his attention deeper into the cave.

"Jake!" shouted Marco from somewhere behind him. "Where are you?"

"Over here," Jake yelled back. "Where are the girls?"

"They were too chicken to come inside."

"Figures," said Jake, who wanted to identify the mysterious noises. He was feeling more manly by the minute. "Hey, I think I heard something scramble up against the cave wall over there."

"Now *I'm* scared," Marco said, his voice trembling.

"Don't worry," Jake answered. "I've got a flashlight somewhere in my backpa—"

Jake's words were cut short by the sound of more scratching and scuffling. Marco jumped up on Jake's back, piggyback style, in a desperate effort to get off the ground. They both went sprawling onto the damp, dark floor of the cave.

"Stop that!" yelled Jake as he lay on the rock floor, trying to catch his breath. "You're tickling my ear."

"I'm not touching your ear," said Marco from somewhere in the darkness several feet away from where Jake lay.

Jake froze. "Then who is?" asked Jake quietly.

"I dunno," said Marco, whose voice now sounded

strange to Jake—like one of the old women sopranos in the church choir. "What does it feel like?"

"It feels hairy and scratchy," Jake answered, feeling much less brave than he had a few moments ago.

"Turn on your flashlight!" Marco shouted.

"I told you, I couldn't find it!" Jake hollered back as he felt around the cold floor of the cave in the darkness.

"It must have rolled out of your backpack when we fell," Marco said.

"You mean, when you knocked me down," Jake corrected. "OUCH!"

"What! What happened?" Marco almost screamed.

"Something scratched my hand!" Jake answered, rubbing at the scratch as he frantically continued to feel around the floor for the flashlight.

"Here it is!" Marco said with relief. "I found it!"

To Jake's great relief, the cave was suddenly illuminated by the soft glow of the flashlight.

"Yes!" said Jake. "Let there be light!"

"And there's the stolen loot," he heard Marco say softly.

11

SECRETS DISCOVERED

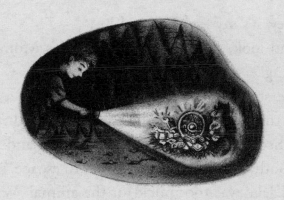

W hat is it?" both girls said at the same time.
They'd entered the cave as soon as they'd
seen the glow of light.

"It looks like we found the thief's hideaway,"
Marco said.

"But he's got a weird guard," Jake answered, his
eyes fixed on the strange sight in front of them.
"What's that?"

There, sitting atop a nest made of sticks and
leaves, coins, car parts, eyeglasses, buckles, spoons, an

old coin purse, and a dozen other shiny objects, sat a chubby mouselike animal with rather large ears, whiskers, and a hairy tail.

"What's he holding in his hands?" whispered Maria.

"Hey, it's my locket!" said Joy.

"And look, there near his foot—it's Mom's wedding ring!"

The startled creature had rolled up in a ball to escape the glow of the light. When that didn't work, he dashed down from his treasure nest and toward the mouth of the cave in an effort to escape.

But Jake was too quick for the animal. With one swift movement, Jake took off his sombrero and threw it on top of the scurrying little fellow, trapping him inside it.

"Now what?" the others asked, looking at Jake, who was standing on the brim of the wiggling sombrero.

"Now we take him to a laboratory for examination," Jake said, with an air of authority.

"But we don't have a laboratory," said Joy as she picked up the locket and ring and put them carefully in her pocket.

"Yes, we do," said Jake. "Mr. Fields set up an animal observation lab at the camp nature center this year."

"Be careful not to squish him," said Maria as Jake rolled the animal up in the wriggling, flexible hat. "He's kind of cute."

"I'm not going to hurt him," Jake replied. "He can breathe through the holes in the straw until we find out what in the world he is."

12

LAB RAT?

A h," said Mr. Fields, examining the Twiblings'
new furry friend. *"Neotoma albigula."*

"Neowhata all biggawhat?" Jake asked as he
looked from Mr. Fields to the small white-footed
creature and back to Mr. Fields again.

"Neotoma albigula," Mr. Fields repeated as he
pushed his glasses up over his balding head to get a
closer look at the captive creature. "Or more com-
monly known as the 'wood rat' or 'pack rat.' This is a
white-throated wood rat. Though they usually live

near the base of a prickly pear cactus, sometimes they'll make their home in rocky crevices—"

"Or caves?" Jake interrupted.

"Looks like this little guy did," said Mr. Fields as he examined the brownish gray animal through the thin metal mesh of its cage.

Birds sang in the branches above the nature center; a grass snake rustled in an empty aquarium nearby. Mr. Fields had worked hard to create a place in the woods surrounding the old cabin where kids could learn by seeing and touching and interacting with the things around them.

"He looks like a big-eared, furry-tailed gerbil," said Joy.

"Well, he *is* part of the rat family, that's for sure," said Mr. Fields. "This species is called pack rats, or sometimes trade rats, because they love to collect objects and bits of material to use in making their nests."

"Like shiny pieces of foil or wedding rings or watches?" asked Marco.

"Precisely," answered Mr. Fields. "They are especially fond of small, bright, shiny objects, which they will readily confiscate."

"Readily what?" Jake asked. He liked Mr. Fields, but sometimes listening to him talk was more confusing than listening to Señor and Señora Garcia talk in Spanish.

"Oh, I'm sorry, Jake. To 'confiscate' means to 'steal.'"

"Our jewel thief!" the four friends cried at once.

"He really hit the big time at our house," Joy laughed. "Finding my locket and Mom's ring, both! He must have crawled in the house through an open window—the one Munchy likes to play in."

"Well, yes," chuckled Mr. Fields. "There's another interesting thing about pack rats. Remember I told you they are also called 'trade rats' sometimes. They not only take things, but they'll often leave an object in place of one they're taking."

"A trade?" asked Maria, leaning closer to the pack rat for a better look.

"Sort of," Mr. Fields explained. "What actually happens is that a pack rat will be carrying one trophy home to his nest, then he'll happen to see something else that seems suddenly more attractive. Of course, he can only carry one thing at a time, so he has to put down one item to pick up the next."

"That must have been what happened with the foil ball and Mr. Grant's watch," said Joy, suddenly understanding the mystery.

"Yeah!" said Jake. "The pack rat must have stolen the watch that day we ran into Mr. Grant and Mr. Zane, and then on the way back to his cave, he stopped off at our house for a quick look around—"

"And decided the candy wrappers were a better deal than the watch!" finished Maria.

The Twiblings laughed at the thought of the mouse-sized burglar with a pea-sized, illogical brain.

Mr. Fields motioned for the kids to follow him up to the front porch of the cabin-office. He took a seat on an old rocker, then reached to pull a textbook from a small bookshelf made from an old split log. "Listen to this," he said to the kids gathered around him on the porch steps and railings. "This author says that the structures built by *Neotoma* are called 'middens.' They are very valuable as a resource to scientists, as they are often built on top of each other by generations of rats. Some of the material stacked up in middens goes back to the earliest recorded days of man."

"Amazing," Joy said.

Hearing the word "amazing" reminded Jake of the strange clearing the Twiblings had discovered. "Mr. Fields, can I ask you something else?"

"Sure, Jake," Mr. Fields said as he put his reading glasses back on top of his balding head. "Shoot."

"Have you ever heard of bouncing ground?"

"Bouncing ground?" Mr. Fields asked with curiosity.

"Yes," said Jake as the others nodded their heads up and down in agreement. "We were walking through the woods near Camp Wanna Banana when suddenly the ground got spongy, like we were walking on a peanut-butter sandwich or something. It was so cool!"

Mr. Fields put his glasses back on his nose and reached around for another textbook. "Jake," he said, flipping through the pages, "it sounds as though you happened upon yet another very interesting finding, indeed. And a rare one at that."

"We did?" Jake asked feeling incredibly important at having found a finding.

"It sounds like you all discovered a quaking bog."

"A quacking dog? No, Mr. Fields, it was soft, mushy, bouncy ground."

Mr. Fields laughed aloud. "Jake, I didn't say a quacking dog—I said a 'quaking bog.'" Mr. Fields grew suddenly thoughtful as he silently reached for a clipboard with paper, then pulled a pencil out of his pocket and began tapping it. "Let's go for a walk in the woods. Jake, if you've discovered what I think you have found…" Mr. Fields hesitated, not finishing his sentence.

"What?" the twins asked excitedly.

"I'd better not say anything until we're sure of what we have."

"Do you think it's a GM?" Jake asked.

Mr. Fields nodded. "Sounds like one of God's Miracles to me. Let's go check it out. But first I'd like to go inside and call a friend of mine to join us. He's an old college buddy, a geologist who just moved to Tall Pines. His opinion could prove to be very helpful in this case."

"What's his name?" asked Joy.

"Rick Zane," came Mr. Field's reply.

13

TREASURE SWAMP

"Look over here, Rick," Mr. Fields spoke with the wonder of a child on Christmas morning as he poked around the edges of the moss-covered bog. "Orchids! Pitcher plants! Sundew! Venus's-flytrap! A gold mine!"

"A gold mine?" asked Jake. "Really?"

"In a manner of speaking," replied Mr. Fields. "This bog is a virtual treasure chest of rare and exotic plants."

Joy touched one of the beautiful, bright orange, yellow, and pink flowers. The blossom closed on her fingers. "Hey, this flower tried to bite me!" she exclaimed.

"Indeed," Mr. Fields explained, "many of these rare flowers are carnivorous. They eat meat."

"Like steak?" asked Jake, his mouth open wide with astonishment. "Or human fingers?"

"No," said Mr. Fields with a grin, "but they do like flies and bugs."

"Wow," Marco said, hardly believing his eyes as a fly landed on the open "mouth" of the Venus's-flytrap, then disappeared as if it had been swallowed. "It's like a science-fiction movie around here. Rats that build nests out of jewelry and money. Flowers that eat bugs. Trampoline ground."

"Rick," Mr. Fields said, "you are the expert in geology, the study of the earth. Tell us about this bog. What is it and how was it formed?"

Rick Zane reached to the middle of the spongy ground with a stick. "First of all," Rick said, "I need to let you kids know that you should be very careful when walking across a bog. If the moss isn't thick enough, you could fall through to the water beneath. But this bog appears to be thick and stable enough to walk across."

"There's water underneath it?" asked Maria.

"Yes," said Rick as he sat down on a nearby log to explain. "Years ago this was a lake that became acidic over time—in other words, a clear pond grew into a thick, souplike swamp. Gradually peat moss grew over the top of the pond, forming a mat, until it was completely covered over."

Mr. Fields nodded and then added his own insight. "The rare plants you see here only grow in bogs like this. From a natural scientist's point of view, this little area of forest you four have found is just like discovering a hoard of jewels."

"A whole forest full of GMs! Would it be worth enough to pay for the taxes my dad owes on Camp Wanna Banana?" Jake asked excitedly. "I've been praying and praying for God to send us some money to save the camp from the bank. Maybe he sent us a swamp instead!"

Rick Zane reached over and tousled Jake's hair. "Jake, I want you to know that I'm sorry about the other day. It's my job to test land, but I hated the thought of seeing this beautiful forest destroyed by Mr. Grant's sawmill."

Jake looked up and smiled at Rick. He'd known

from the first time he'd seen Rick's kind eyes that this man had a good heart.

Mr. Fields nodded in their direction and said, "I think God may have just answered your prayer, son." He paused and looked around him, breathing in the scent of earth and forest. "And mine as well," he said softly.

14

MONKEYS, MYSTERIES, AND MIRACLES

One month later, Jake, riding Brick, led a group of laughing, talking, and exhausted campers on horseback into the woods near the edge of Camp Wanna Banana.

"Are we there yet, Jake?" one of the first-grade campers asked excitedly.

"Almost," replied Jake. "Look way up there ahead on the trail. Can you read the sign hung between those two giant oak trees?"

A bright little girl with a missing tooth spoke up.

"It sayth, 'Nature Ob…Obthervatory,'" she lisped. "What doth that mean?"

Jake looked around him and smiled broadly. "A nature observatory is a special place to come look at the secrets of God's creation."

"Will we really get to walk on bouncy ground?" asked a boy who'd heard about the mysterious, amazing bog.

"And see flowers that eat flies?" asked another camper wearing a bright yellow Camp Wanna Banana T-shirt.

"And a rat that collects coins?" a young girl chimed in.

"Why don't you ask our camp naturalist, Mr. Fields," Mr. Bigsley's voice called out from somewhere in front of the trail riders.

Mr. Bigsley pointed toward Mr. Fields, who was walking out of Pack Rat Cave into the clearing. The science teacher brushed the dirt off his khakis as he walked and shouted, "Well hello, kids!" Then he turned and hollered into the cave. "Hey—Joy, Marco, and Maria! We have company!" Jake's friends came out of the cave, blinking as their eyes adjusted to the sunlight.

So much had happened in the few weeks since the Twiblings had discovered this wonderful spot in the forest. Soon after the Twiblings led their science teacher and Mr. Zane to the bog and the cave, Mr. Fields contacted God's Natural Treasures. When the organization heard about the rare quaking bog and about the possibility of Camp Wanna Banana being turned into a sawmill, they saved the property from going to the bank by donating the needed tax money. In return for the generosity of God's Natural Treasures, Mr. Bigsley happily promised to preserve the bog, to keep it just the way his children found it, so that scientists and other children could always come and enjoy what God had made.

It seemed that everyone was happy. Everyone, that is, except Mr. Grant, who would never get to build his sawmill anywhere near Camp Wanna Banana. (Though he did receive an apology from Jake and got back his slightly pack-rat-scratched gold watch.)

During the school year, Mr. Fields would also be allowed to bring his classes out to the conservatory for special field trips. He was thrilled to be able to introduce his students to the marvels of nature outside of books, beyond the walls of the classroom. In fact, he had been praying for many years that the Lord would provide him and his students with a nature science lab.

Mr. Fields opened his mouth to begin the tour when something—or someone—came swinging out of a tree above the heads of the campers and landed splat in the middle of the bog. The "thing" was short and hairy and curled up in a ball.

"What's that?" the children cried.

"Ith it the pack rat?" the little girl with the lisp asked.

Jake and Joy laughed. "No, it's not a pack rat," Joy explained, recognizing her furry friend right away. "Just a little monkey taking what doesn't belong to her again."

Munch-Munch held five Golden Nugget chocolate bars tightly between her two small hands, and she was screeching with delight.

"Give those to me," Joy told her pet. "Remember how sick you got last time?"

Munchy shook her head and screamed some more. The campers started laughing at the funny monkey's antics.

"Munch-Munch Bigsley!" Joy repeated, more firmly and loudly. "Give me those candy bars right this minute."

This time Munch-Munch turned her big sad eyes on her master and reluctantly handed over the chocolate loot.

"Good girl," said Joy, picking up her monkey and softly petting her small hairy back. "Now you may have one candy bar for obeying. But just one. This way you can enjoy a treat without getting sick."

Jake smiled at the monkey who was finally learning a hard lesson. Even though it was hard for Munchy to use self-control, her small monkey brain somehow knew that her loving master knew best. And having been sick for three days, Munchy never wanted to experience an awful tummyache again.

Jake reached over to take Munch-Munch from Joy and give her a monkey-back ride around the nature observatory, which was full of excited campers. Looking at Munchy, he realized he, too, had learned a valuable lesson about self-control this summer.

He'd tried to worry about problems that were too big for him. And, like eating seven candy bars in one sitting, it had made him feel sick. Whenever he tried to fix problems without asking for God's help, he ended up with a tummy full of worry and made one mistake after another. He'd lost control with his father's banker. He'd accused his best friend of stealing. But as Jake's father encouraged Jake to relax, to trust and pray and follow God's path—to take each day one bite at a time—God had answered his prayers in the most surprising way.

"Hey!" one of the children interrupted Jake's thoughts with a loud yell. "I'm missing my bag of pennies! Who took my coins?"

"My gold hair barrette is gone, too!" shouted another child. "I just laid it down on that log over there for a minute."

Jake winked at his fellow Twiblings, who smiled knowingly at the confusion. Together the foursome led a group of curious children into the cave of the mysterious pint-sized jewel thief of Camp Wanna Banana.

THE TWIBLINGS' ACTIVITY PAGES

*Always ask an adult to help you
with these crafts and recipes!*

SEÑORA GARCIA'S TORTILLA GOBBLER SNACKS

2 dinner plates
1 flour tortilla
a handful of grated cheese
picante sauce or salsa
plastic wrap or a paper towel (optional)

Place a flour tortilla on a dinner plate. Sprinkle a small handful of grated cheese down the middle. Top with any kind of picante sauce. Roll up the tortilla and cover the plate with another upside down plate (like a flying saucer)—or with a loose paper towel or plastic wrap. Microwave for one minute or until cheese has melted. Mmmmm, good.

THE PACK RAT'S TREASURE NEST

See how many items you can find in his nest.

eyeglasses	pliers	transistor radio
belt buckle	AA battery	paper clip
lipstick	diamond ring	necklace
nickel	light bulb	screwdriver
quarter	wrist watch	spoon
crescent wrench	key	
CD	comb	

JAKE'S ADVENTURE BOX

a cigar box, or other sturdy box with a lid
glue
old magazines
scissors
varnish, shellac, or Puzzle Preserver

Cut out pictures and words that you like from old magazines. Glue them all over the box until the box is completely covered. When it's dry, paint your adventure box with a clear coat of varnish or shellac. Puzzle Preserver works great too! Use your Adventure Box to store small treasures that remind you of places you've been—seashells, arrowheads, coins, trinkets, napkins, rocks—anything to help you remember your special day!

CRITTER KEEPER

an oatmeal carton
an old pair of clean pantyhose
a rubber band

Remove the lid of the cardboard oatmeal carton. Carefully cut a big "window" out of the side of the box—plenty big enough for you to see your critter and for the critter to get air. Slide the carton into one leg of the pantyhose and pull the pantyhose tight. Tie off the pantyhose with a rubber band and cut off the excess nylon. When you find a bug, undo the rubber band, and put your critter in the critter keeper along with some water, leaves, dirt—and maybe even slices of apple or potato. Watch your critter for a couple of days, then let him go—and find a new critter to observe!

Author's Note

My own adventurer husband, Scott, gave me the idea for this story. Like Mr. Bigsley, Scott works with nature, builds giant tree houses, and manages camps for children. One day while riding on horseback at a camp that Scott oversees in East Texas, he happened upon a piece of "mushy ground" filled with beautiful plants. Soon, nature scientists came out and declared it a rare find—a quaking bog, just like the one Jake and Joy discovered.

The characters of Jake and Joy are based on real twins in my neighborhood named Nicky and Lindsey Patton. Nicky is always ready for adventure and comes over to play in what he calls our "bamboo forest." Lindsey, who loves to read, actually invented the word *twiblings* one day while we were riding bikes together. I thought it was a wonderful word—a mixture of "siblings" and "twins"—and asked her if I could use it in my next book. She said that would be just fine with her, so I did. Thanks, Lindsey.

Most of my stories begin with real events. Then I mix them with a bit of imagination and—poof!—a

book is soon filled with words that I hope will enter-
tain kids like you who read them.

May you have many adventures, and may God
bless you with friends!

Love,

Becky Freeman

P.S. Come visit my Kids' Corner Web site at
www.beckyfreeman.com!